# MINE'S THE BEST

An Early I CAN READ Book ®

by CROSBY BONSALL

**HarperCollins**Publishers

Early I Can Read Book is a registered trademark
of HarperCollins Publishers.

MINE'S THE BEST
Copyright © 1973 by Crosby Bonsall.
Printed in the United States of America. For information address
HarperCollins Children's Books, a division of HarperCollins Publishers,
10 East 53rd Street, New York, NY 10022.

Library of Congress Catalog Card Number: 72-9863
ISBN 0-06-020577-6
ISBN 0-06-020578-4 (lib. bdg.)

# MINE'S THE BEST

"Mine is the best."

"It is not.

Mine is."

"Mine has more spots."

"It does not.

Mine has."

"Well, mine is bigger."

"It is not.

Mine is."

"Mine can stand up."

"Mine can too."

"Mine can sit

on my head."

"Mine can sit

on MY head."

"I can ride mine."

"I can ride mine better."

"Yours is sick."

"So is yours."

"Yours is very sick."

"So is yours."

"Yours is dead."

"Yours is dead too."

"It's all your fault."

"No, It's all YOUR fault."

"Let go of my pants."

"Let go of my hat."

"She thinks
she's smart!"

"I hate her."

"Ours was the best."